Donna and Dermot
Heal

By Hilda Kalap
and Jacob Artemenko

Hilda Kalap is based in Devon, UK and is an author, healer and teacher and 'Donna and Dermot Heal' is her second picture book. She has been writing and healing since she was a child.

Hilda has two daughters and enjoys spending time on Dartmoor, on the Cornish coastline and in nature in general. She loves travelling and has visited over 60 countries.

Jacob Artemenko (Art) is an illustrator based in the Ukraine. Originally studying to be a lawyer, he switched to illustration after realising this was his passion. He has illustrated many works including picture books. He likes travelling and exploring new cultures.

Dedication

This book is dedicated to the healers that are transforming lives all over the world, bringing safety where there is fear, offering hope where there is despair.

Donna and Dermot

Heal

Acknowledgements

Hilda would like to acknowledge: Jacob Artemenko (Art) for his remarkable illustrations, the Totnes Natural Health Centre, Ola Chiropractic, Rowcroft Hospice, Natura Training Institute, the National Centre for Integrative Medicine, Titanya and Dondi Dahlin of Innersource, and Mike the Pirate, the man who makes me laugh the most.

Donna and her dog Dermot were walking home from school when they saw Charlotte, an older girl from Donna's school. She was limping and looked in pain.

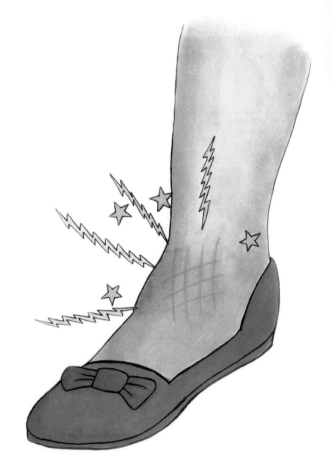

"What's the matter?"asked Donna.
"My ankle hurts, I think I've twisted it,"
gasped Charlotte and sure enough her
poor ankle was swelling up.

Donna knew how to heal using the energy from her hands. Her mother was a healer and had always told Donna that everyone is born with the power to heal. She had shown her how easy it was.

Donna asked Charlotte if she could put healing energy into her ankle using her hands. Charlotte was not sure at first but she liked and trusted Donna so she said "yes". Donna smiled and put her hands on Charlotte's ankle.

Donna imagined the energy coming into her hands from the huge force of energy in the sky, meaning it was endless and she would not get tired. She imagined her head, then her hands and then her whole body filling with the golden light of this endless energy.

Donna pictured the swelling going down, coming out of the end of Charlotte's toes until her ankle was back to normal. She pictured the pain as little sad blue faces that turned into happy orange ones until all the pain was gone.

Donna's hands felt very warm, then tingly and then normal. After a while Charlotte's face was relaxed and peaceful, "my ankle barely hurts at all though it's still a bit swollen," she said. "Thank you ever so much!" Charlotte stood up and could walk without help. She waved goodbye to Donna and Dermot and headed home.

Donna and Dermot did a high five. When they reached home Donna told her mum what had happened. "That's wonderful Donna, well done for helping Charlotte!" Donna's mother explained a bit more to Donna about Chi. Chi is the energy force that flows through everyone. To be in good health the energy should flow well and be strong.

Donna's mum explained that when Chi is not strong or gets blocked then you might start to feel tired and unwell. Chi is not just in the body but in the thoughts and feelings too.

That night Donna did some healing on herself by placing her hands on her forehead and her tummy. She did this most nights as it helped her to sleep well and to feel calm and happy.

She also did some healing on Dermot. He loved the energy to be beamed onto his tummy, his head and his legs. Dermot fell asleep almost straight away.

Donna's best friend Ayesha came to play the next day. Ayesha had broken her arm a few weeks before. Now it was out of its cast and getting better.

Ayesha was the school's table tennis champion and there was a competition coming up. She wanted her arm to get better more quickly.

"I will massage your arm," said Donna.

Donna's mum had taught her to massage.

After the massage was over, Ayesha wriggled her fingers and they moved lightly and easily about. Ayesha gave Donna a hug. "Your hands have magic powers," she said.

"It's really easy to do," said Donna, "I'll teach you if you want."

"Yes, when my arm feels a bit stronger," said Ayesha.

It was the day of the school table tennis competition. Ayesha had had lots of massages and her arm was feeling good. She walked away with the school table tennis cup for the second year in a row. "Ayesha Ayesha!" everyone chanted.

After school Ayesha and another friend, Emily, came to Donna's house for dinner. Donna's mum had made tuna sandwiches cut in the shape of fish and fairy cakes with table tennis bats on the top.

The girls, with Dermot beside them, feasted until they were full. After dinner Donna showed Ayesha and Emily how to bring the healing energy into their hands. They practised on each other and Dermot.

Then Donna showed them how to massage the feet. Ayesha practised on Donna and Emily practised on Donna's brother George.

After the massage they felt so full of energy
that they danced around the house, and
ran into the garden barefoot to watch the
sun go down.

Next morning the sunflowers were out and it felt as if summer was in full flow. Donna was worried about sunburn. She remembered getting burnt last summer. Dermot was an expert on essential oils – oils from plants that are used for healing.

Dermot went to his kennel. From inside he fetched a book and a box with small bottles of oils in it.

He made a sunspray by mixing some water with a few drops of lavender and peppermint oil.
"This will do the trick," motioned Dermot with his paw and handed the bottle to Donna.

Donna was also worried she might get insect bites or bee stings on her school camping trip.
She was heading off tomorrow.

No problem for Dermot. Before long he'd brought out a bottle of witch hazel and some lavender and chamomile oils. He handed all of them to Donna to pack for her trip.

Donna patted Dermot on the head. "Clever dog, where would I be without you?" she asked.

All Donna needed now was a potion for cuts and scrapes.

"Easy," thought Dermot. He mixed some raw honey with tea tree oil and handed Donna a small container.

"I'll miss you Dermot," said Donna. "I wish you were coming too." She would be away for five days and walk for miles across a moor where wild ponies roamed. Every night her class would camp under the night stars.

On the day of the school camp, Donna kissed Dermot goodbye. Her mum helped Donna with her rucksack and gave her a big hug and kiss. "It'll be quiet at home without you. Have a safe trip," she said.

That evening at the campsite Donna, Ayesha and Emily saw a queue had formed outside their tent. "Heard you could help with aching feet," said Ollie.

"Word sure spreads quickly round the school," thought Donna.

"Don't worry we're right behind you," said Ayesha and Emily, "Let the healing begin!"

THE END

Donna and her dog Dermot show the power of natural health – see how easy energy healing is and learn about massage and essential oils. Donna and Dermot help heal twisted ankles, aching feet and insect bites in this second book in the Donna and Dermot series of picture books.

Printed in Poland
by Amazon Fulfillment
Poland Sp. z o.o., Wrocław

89420908R00020